D0070669

First American Edition. Copyright © 1995 The Walt Disney Company.
All rights reserved under international copyright conventions.
Published in the United States by Grolier Enterprises Inc.,
Danbury, Connecticut. Originally published in Denmark by Egmont
Gruppen, Copenhagen. ISBN: 0-7172-8496-4
Manufactured in the United States of America.   B C D 6 7 8 9

DISNEY'S

Simba and Nala Help Bomo

GROLIER
BOOK CLUB EDITION

It was a hot day on the African plain.
Zebras were grazing on the green grass.
Giraffes were searching the treetops for
tender leaves.

Elephants were returning from the watering hole.

And Kula, a Cape buffalo, had just awakened from his nap. It was time for lunch.

None of the animals noticed little Simba.
The lion cub was hunting.
He crept up behind Kula.
He pounced!

Then Simba roared with all his might!

But Kula never stopped eating. Simba didn't scare him one bit.

In fact, none of the animals was afraid of the tiny lion cub.

"Simba," Kula said, "it's too hot to play silly cub games."

The buffalo swung his tail. Poor Simba was knocked to the ground.

"Ouch!" the cub cried.

The little lion cub watched as the animals wandered off.

"How will I ever become a great lion king if no one is afraid of me?" Simba wondered.

Simba began to walk home. Suddenly he heard a familiar voice call him.

"Simba! There you are. I've been looking all over for you." It was his best friend, Nala.

"Do you want to play a game?" she asked.

"No," said Simba. He sighed. "I don't feel like playing."

"Please," Nala pleaded. "We could play tag."

She continued,
"Or hide-and-seek.
Or leapfrog."

"I said, I don't feel
like playing," Simba
answered.

"What's the
matter?"
asked Nala
"Are you
feeling sick?"

"No," replied Simba. "But I'm tired of silly cubs' games."

"I thought you liked games," said Nala.

"Not any longer." Simba sighed.
"No one takes me seriously.
I'll never be a good lion king," he added.

Just then the two cubs heard a strange noise.
"What's that?" asked Nala.
"I don't know," Simba answered. "Let's find out."
The two friends followed the noise. It led
them to the edge of a muddy pond.

"Over here!"
Nala whispered.
    The cubs crept
closer and closer.
    They peeked
through the tall grass . . .

. . . and saw a baby elephant.

"Help!" the elephant called. "I'm stuck in the mud!"

"What happened?" Nala asked.

"I wandered away from my mother. She told me to stay close to her, but I didn't listen. I didn't think I'd get into this mess," the elephant said sadly.

Simba knew all about getting into trouble. He felt sorry for the baby elephant. "What's your name?" he asked.

"My name is Bomo. Can you help me?"

"Don't worry. I'm the future lion king. I can get you out of the mud," Simba assured him.

Simba and Nala tried pulling from behind.
"Ouch!" Bomo cried. "That hurts!"
They pulled and pulled. But Bomo didn't move at all.

So Simba tried pulling from the front.
"Ouch! My trunk is long enough already!"
Bomo shouted. But he still hadn't moved.
Then Nala had an idea.

"Let's use that log to get
    Bomo out," she said to Simba.
    The two cubs rolled the log to
        the edge of the pond.

They slid one end of the log under Bomo.
"Pull the other end down," Nala told Simba.
"That should lift Bomo up!"

Simba pulled and pulled with all his might.

"I don't think this is working either," said Bomo. "I'm too heavy."

"I can do it," Simba grunted. "Just . . . a . . . little . . . harder."

SPLAT! The lion cub fell into the mud.

Bomo and Nala laughed.

"Simba, this is no time to take a mud bath," teased Nala.

"Very funny," Simba snapped. He crawled out of the pond. "Got any other bright ideas?"

Nala looked at Simba's muddy face.

"As a matter of fact, I have. Wait here," Nala
called as she ran off.

Nala returned with a mouth full of leaves.

"What are you going to do with those?" Simba asked.

Nala smiled. "You'll see."

Suddenly Nala flipped Simba onto his back.
She began sticking the leaves all around his face.
The mud held them in place.

"Stop that!" Simba shouted. "I don't want to
play silly games. I have to get Bomo out of the mud."

"You will," Nala promised when she finished. "Now you look like a mighty lion king."

"I look mighty foolish," grumbled Simba.

"You're too small to pull that log down by yourself," said Nala.

Simba looked at his friend sadly. She was right.

"But you *are* big enough to scare up some help," she continued.

The cubs went to the
edge of the great plain.

Then Nala whispered the rest of her plan to Simba.

Simba did as he was told. He rushed out onto
the plain.

"ROAR!!" It was the loudest roar Simba had
ever made.

The other animals were frightened! They had never seen such a strange-looking creature before! The zebras ran away as fast as they could.
So did the giraffes and the antelope.
Even Kula, the great Cape buffalo, ran away!

"Chase them to the pond!" Nala shouted.

So Simba chased the herd of animals. He roared and snapped at their heels. At last the other animals were afraid of the future lion king!

Nala's plan was working. Simba chased the animals all the way to the muddy pond.

Some of the animals
ran around the pond.
Some of the animals
leaped over the pond.

And, just as Nala planned,
one animal jumped . . .

. . . right into the pond!
Kula landed on the end of the log.
And when the heavy buffalo
pushed the log down, Bomo flew up!

The cubs had helped Bomo get out of the mud!

Bomo landed in some soft bushes. He was very happy to be unstuck.

"Thanks. You saved my life," Bomo said.

"It's Simba you should really thank," Nala told him. "If he hadn't been so brave and scary, those animals would never have run this way."

"I was pretty brave, wasn't I?" Simba said proudly. "Maybe I will be a good lion king after all!"

Nala nodded. Then she started pulling the leaves off her friend.

"It's late," Bomo said. "I have to get back home."

"So do we," Nala told him. She yawned.
"But all that running has made me tired."

"Well, a future king doesn't get tired. But I
wouldn't mind a nap," admitted Simba.

"Why don't you both climb on my back?"
said Bomo. "It's the least I can do."

So Simba and Nala rode home on Bomo's
back. They couldn't wait to tell their friends about
their rescue of Bomo, the baby elephant.